# AREN'T YOU COMING TOO?

woof

# AREN'T YOU COMING TOO?

by Eve Rice

✳

illustrated by
Nancy Winslow Parker

 Greenwillow Books, New York

Black pen, watercolor paints, and colored pencils were
used for the full-color art. The text type is Weidemann.

Text copyright © 1988 by Eve Rice
Illustrations copyright © 1988 by Nancy Winslow Parker
All rights reserved. No part of this book
may be reproduced or utilized in any form
or by any means, electronic or mechanical,
including photocopying, recording or by
any information storage and retrieval
system, without permission in writing
from the Publisher, Greenwillow Books,
a division of William Morrow & Company, Inc.,
105 Madison Avenue, New York, N.Y. 10016.
Printed in Hong Kong by South China Printing Co.
First Edition    10 9 8 7 6 5 4 3 2 1

Library of Congress Cataloging-in-Publication Data

Rice, Eve.
Aren't you coming too?
Summary: Amy watches as everyone leaves the house
and as neighbors are busy in the street, but when
Grandpa finally comes Amy goes out too.
[1. Grandfathers—Fiction]
I. Parker, Nancy Winslow, ill.    II. Title.
PZ7.R3622Ar  1988    [E]    86-33506
ISBN 0-688-06446-9
ISBN 0-688-06447-7 (lib. bdg.)

One morning early…

Amy watches out the window as Dee and Sam and Maryanne go off to school.

And Lily shouts,
"Wait for me!
 I'm coming too!"

She runs downstairs—
and then she's gone.

Amy sees a truck pull up

and men get out
and lift big pails.

The paperboy
goes pedaling past,

Then Papa puts on his hat and
swoops up Amy in his arms.
"I'm off to work," he says.

He waves goodbye
all the way
down the steps.

Mama puts some
papers in her case
and winds her watch.

While out the window,
Amy hears a motor start,
*Vrooooom!*

*Vrooooom!*
And all the pigeons fly at once.

"Aren't you coming too?" they seem to call as Mr. Webb, hurrying by, nods hello.

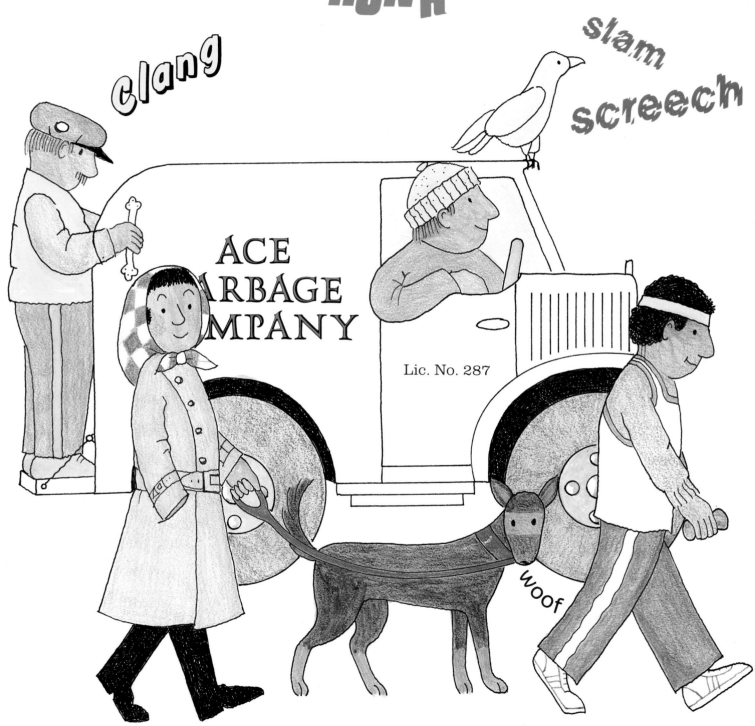

But what is that down the
block? Someone is coming,

Grandpa hugs Amy.
"Today is our day," he says.
"What shall we do? Visit
the animals in the park?"

"Oh yes!" Amy says. Mama kisses her goodbye and goes to work.

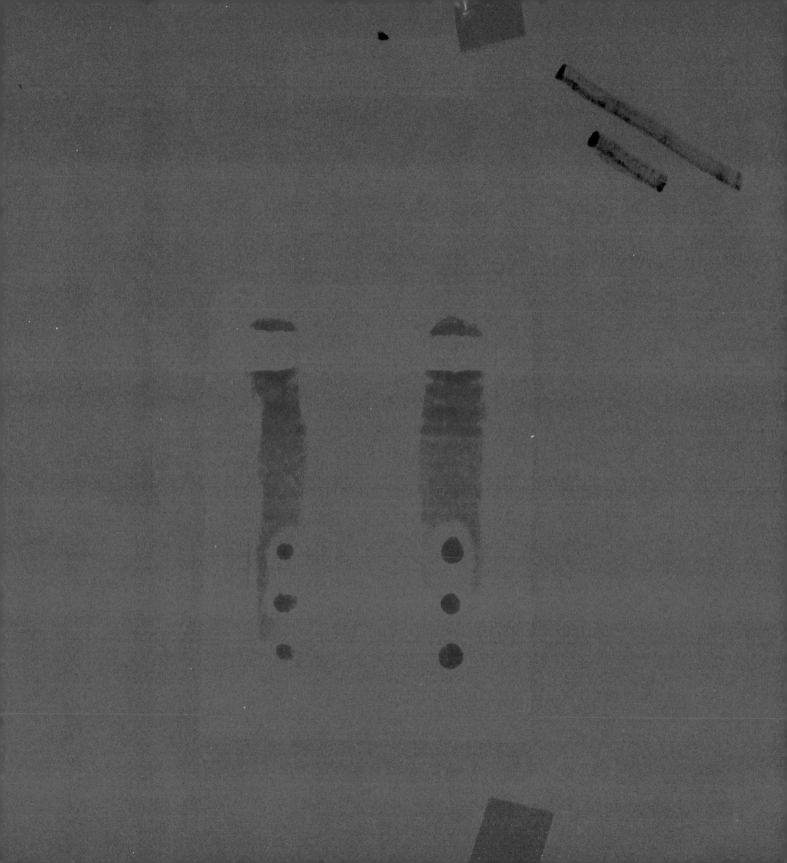

PIC                              c.1
RIC                           056993

     RICE, EVE

  Aren't You Coming Too?